The Big
What Are
Friends For?
Storybook

KINGFISHER
An imprint of Kingfisher Publications Plc
New Penderel House, 283-288 High Holborn,
London WC1V 7HZ
www.kingfisherpub.com

First published by Kingfisher 2002
4 6 8 10 9 7 5 3
3TR(PREM)/0603/TWP/FR/150SEM

Stories first published by Kingfisher in three separate volumes:
What Are Friends For? (1998)
What Will I Do Without You? (1999)
Will You Forgive Me? (2001)

A CIP catalogue record for this book is available from the British Library.

ISBN 0 7534 0729 9

Printed in Singapore

THE BIG
WHAT ARE
FRIENDS FOR?
STORYBOOK

SALLY GRINDLEY

ILLUSTRATED BY PENNY DANN

KINGFISHER

Contents

What Are Friends For?

Jefferson Bear and Figgy Twosocks went
walking one day in the sunny green woods.
"JB," asked Figgy Twosocks,
"are you my friend?"

"Yes," said Jefferson Bear. "I am your friend, and you are my friend."

"But what is a friend for?" asked Figgy Twosocks.

"Well…" said Jefferson Bear. "A friend is for playing."

"Goody," said Figgy Twosocks. "Let's play hide-and-seek."

"All right," said Jefferson Bear. "You hide first."

Figgy Twosocks hid in a hollow tree.

Jefferson Bear looked everywhere,

but couldn't find her.

When it was his turn,
he hid behind a tree stump.
Figgy Twosocks
found him straightaway.
"You're better at this
than me," said
Jefferson Bear.

"I'll help you this time,"
said Figgy Twosocks. She hid
under a pile of leaves,
but left the tip of her
tail showing.

The next day, Figgy Twosocks asked, "JB, what else is a friend for?"

"Well," said Jefferson Bear, scratching his head. "A friend is for sharing."

"We share, don't we, JB? We share the sky and the hills and the trees."

"Yes," said Jefferson Bear, "we share lots of things."

"What do *best* friends share?" asked Figgy Twosocks.

"Well," said Jefferson Bear,
"best friends share their favourite things."
Figgy Twosocks thought about this, then darted
off through the woods. When she came back,
she was tugging an enormous
bramble covered with
blackberries.

"Would you like some, JB?"
she said. "Blackberries
are my favourites.
Yummy, aren't they?"

"De–licious," said Jefferson Bear.

17

That afternoon, loud squeals woke
Jefferson Bear from his sleep.

yelp! yelp! yelp! yelp!

yelp! yelp! yelp! yelp!

"I'm coming," he bellowed.
"What's the matter?"

He found Figgy Twosocks lying
on the ground.

"You've got a thorn in your foot.
Keep still and I'll take it out."

"Will it hurt?" whimpered
Figgy Twosocks.

"I'll be as gentle as I can,"
said Jefferson Bear.

Figgy Twosocks was frightened when she saw her friend's sharp teeth, but she lay still. Jefferson Bear closed his teeth round the thorn and pulled.

As soon as it was out, Figgy Twosocks jumped up and pranced around.

"Thank you, JB," she said.
"Thank you for helping me."
"That's what friends are for,"
said Jefferson Bear.

The next afternoon, Jefferson Bear was dozing in the sun. Figgy Twosocks wanted to play. She crept up behind him and yelled…

"BOO!"

Jefferson Bear nearly jumped out of his
wobbly fur. Figgy Twosocks ran round and round
squealing, "Made you jump! Made you jump!"
and laughed and waved her tail.

Jefferson Bear
didn't think it was funny.

"Go away, Figgy Twosocks," he said.
"You have made me cross."

"But I want to play," said Figgy Twosocks.

"And I want to sleep," said Jefferson Bear.
"A big brown bear needs his sleep."

"And a little red fox needs her play,"
said Figgy Twosocks.

"Then go and play somewhere else,"
said Jefferson Bear.

"You're not my friend any more," said
Figgy Twosocks sadly, and she trudged off.

When Jefferson Bear woke up next morning, he felt sorry he had upset his friend.

"I'll play with her today," he said to himself.

But Figgy Twosocks stayed away.

Jefferson Bear began to worry. He went to
her den and called, "Figgy Twosocks,
it's Jefferson Bear.
Are you all right?"

There was no reply.

Jefferson Bear's worry grew. He walked to the edge of the river and called again, "Where are you, Figgy Twosocks?"

But there was no reply.

Jefferson Bear's worry grew bigger. He
walked through the woods calling, "Come out,
Figgy Twosocks, it's me,
Jefferson Bear."

But there was still no reply.

At last, he came to the hollow tree where they had played hide-and-seek. He saw the tip of a tail sticking out.

"Figgy Twosocks, is that you?" he called. "It's JB."

He listened and thought
he heard something.

He listened again and was
sure he heard a sniff.

The sniff grew
louder and
louder and louder
until it turned
into a **great**

big

33

SOB.

"Figgy Twosocks?" said Jefferson Bear.

"Yes," sobbed Figgy Twosocks.

"Please come out," said Jefferson Bear.

"I miss you."

"I'm sorry, JB," said Figgy Twosocks.

"I didn't mean to make you cross."

"And I'm sorry I was so grumpy,"
said Jefferson Bear. "Let's go and play."

"JB," sniffed Figgy Twosocks,
"does that mean you're still my friend?"

"Of course I'm still your friend,"
said Jefferson Bear. "A friend is for ever."

What Will I
Do Without
You?

Winter was on its way. Jefferson Bear was fat
and his fur wobbled more than ever.

"Shall we go for our walk?" asked Figgy Twosocks.

"No time to walk, Figgy," said Jefferson Bear.
"I need to eat. I'm getting ready to hibernate."
"What's hibernate?" asked Figgy.
"Hibernate is what big brown bears
do in the winter," said Jefferson Bear.
"It's when I go to sleep and
don't wake up until Spring."

"But what will I do without you?" asked Figgy.

"I'll be back before you know it," said Jefferson Bear.

"I don't want you to go," sulked Figgy Twosocks.

The air turned frosty.

"Time for bed," yawned Jefferson Bear.

"Don't go yet," said Figgy Twosocks.

"I'm sorry little friend –
a big brown bear needs his sleep."

Jefferson Bear hugged her tight and disappeared into his cave.

"I'll miss you, JB," called Figgy.

PIT
PAT
PIT
PAT
PIT
PAT
PIT

Next morning, it was snowing. Figgy had never seen snow before. She ran to tell Jefferson Bear.

"JB, are you asleep yet?" she called.
A rumbly snore echoed from deep
inside his cave.

Figgy kicked at the snow.
"What good is snow when your
best friend isn't there to share it?"

BIFF! BIFF! BIFF!

Figgy's brothers were
having a snowball fight.

"Can I play?" Figgy Twosocks asked.
"If you want," said Big Smudge.

"Take this," said Floppylugs.

BIFF!

"Stop it!" Figgy squealed. "That hurts."
"You wanted to play," they said,
and ran off laughing.
"You wouldn't do that if JB
was here," she cried.

Then Figgy Twosocks
had an idea . . .

All day long she pushed and patted the snow.

All day long she rolled and scooped and shaped it.

At last, she found
three black stones and
a little twig.

She stood back.

49

"Every time I look at my Big White Snow Bear, I will think of JB," she said.

Pow! Pow! Figgy Twosocks woke the next morning to find Big Smudge and Floppylugs pelting the Snow Bear.

"Stop it!" she cried. "Leave him alone."

"Crybaby, crybaby," called her brothers, skipping away.

Figgy Twosocks felt very lonely. She sobbed a great big sob.

Then she began to feel cross.
If JB was her friend, how could
he leave her for so long?
    PIFF! – she threw a snowball
at the Snow Bear.
    PIFF! – and another.
And another – PIFF!

"Hey, don't do that. You'll spoil it," called a voice.

It was Hoptail, the squirrel.

"JB's not my friend any more,"
said Figgy Twosocks.

"Why not?" asked Hoptail.

"He's not here when I
need him."

"But he needs his sleep,"
said Hoptail. "And I need some
help. I must find the nuts
I buried in the autumn."

Hoptail pointed to places where she thought her food was hidden.

Figgy Twosocks dug through the snow and earth. "One for you!" she squealed, each time she dug up a nut.

"One for me!" she squealed, each time she dug up a worm.

Day after day, more snow fell. Figgy Twosocks and Hoptail ran through the woods making patterns with their pawprints.

They broke off icicles and watched them melt through their paws.

And together they rebuilt the Big White Snow Bear.

At the end of each day, Figgy Twosocks went to see the Big White Snow Bear.
"I hope JB won't mind me having another friend," she said.

Little by little, the days grew warmer.

"The Snow Bear is melting!" cried Figgy.
"What's happening?"

"Spring is coming," said Hoptail.

Suddenly, Big Smudge and Floppylugs appeared.

They clambered
on to the Snow Bear
and pushed –
HEAVE . . .

WHOOSH!

The head of the Snow Bear
rolled down the hill.

GRRR!

"OUCH, that hurt," growled a
great big voice.

Big Smudge and Floppylugs ran away.

There was Jefferson Bear, rubbing his nose.
"That's a fine welcome back," he said.

"JB!" squealed Figgy. "Oh, I've missed you so much. I built a Snow Bear to remind me of you and I hope you don't mind, I've –"

"Yes?" said Jefferson Bear. "I've made a new friend – this is Hoptail."

Jefferson Bear laughed. "Slow down, Figgy. Let's all go for a walk and you can tell me just what you did without me."

Will You Forgive Me?

Jefferson Bear was up a tree eating honey.
  "Save some for our midnight feast, JB,"
called Figgy Twosocks.

Just then, Figgy's brothers pranced by.
"Hey, look at this knobbly stick!"
said Big Smudge.

"That's JB's tickling stick," cried Figgy.
"Put it down. You might break it."

"Scaredy-cat!" jeered Big Smudge,
and he threw the stick in the air.

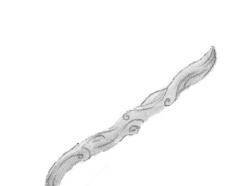

Floppylugs threw
it higher still.

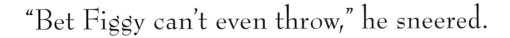

"Bet Figgy can't even throw," he sneered.

"Bet I can," said Figgy Twosocks crossly.
She grabbed the stick . . .

and threw it.

Up, up, up it went . . . .

"OUCH!"

It hit Jefferson Bear on the head.

Then Big Smudge caught the stick. "Let's hide it," he said, and the brothers ran off, sniggering.

Jefferson Bear scrambled down.
"Something hit me on the head,"
he said to Figgy Twosocks.
"Did it?" whispered Figgy.
"Yes, it did," growled Jefferson Bear.
"Now, what I need is a jolly good
scratch. Where's my tickling stick?"

Figgy looked at the ground. "I don't know, JB," she said, and her ears went pink and her nose went all twitchy.

"Well I shall be very cross if it doesn't turn up," said Jefferson Bear, looking at Figgy closely.

Figgy Twosocks rushed off to look for the stick.

She looked in her brothers' den . . .

She looked all along the river bank . . .

She looked in the hollow tree . . .

"What's the matter, Figgy Twosocks?" cried a voice.

It was Hoptail.

"JB's lost his tickling stick, and it's all my fault," said Figgy. "I must find it!"

"Won't any old stick do?" asked Hoptail.

"No," said Figgy. "It's JB's favourite. It's got bumps and knobbles in all the right places, he says."

"Perhaps you should tell Jefferson Bear
what happened," said Hoptail, gently.
"Then he won't be my friend any more and
we won't have our midnight feast," wailed Figgy.

Figgy Twosocks trudged
through the woods.

"BOO!"

Figgy spun round and saw
Jefferson Bear scratching his
back against a tree.

"I just can't get to all the little places without
my tickling stick," he grumbled.

Figgy felt her ears begin to blush
and her nose begin to twitch.
She didn't like that feeling.
She wanted to tell JB
what had happened.

"JB . . ." she began. "I . . . I've got to go!"
And she ran off, just as he was saying,
"What about our feast?"

Figgy ran and ran . . .

and bumped into Buncle the badger.

"Watch out!" grumbled Buncle.
"Sorry," said Figgy. Then she saw
that Buncle was carrying a knobbly stick.

"You've found it!" she cried excitedly.

"Found what?" said Buncle.

"JB's tickling stick," said Figgy.

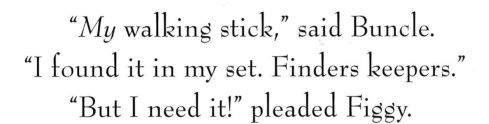

"*My* walking stick," said Buncle.
"I found it in my set. Finders keepers."
"But I need it!" pleaded Figgy.

"Well, I might swap it for something," said
Buncle. "Mmm, yes . . . what about some honey?"

"Where will I find honey?" cried Figgy.
Then she remembered Jefferson Bear's tree.

Figgy Twosocks was
terrified of climbing trees.
"I've got to do it," she
said to herself. "If I don't
get his stick back, JB will
never forgive me."

She began to climb.
Up and up she went
- her knees began to
knock.

Higher and higher - her
head began to feel funny.

She saw the bees' nest
just above her.

She saw the ground
way down below her.

"Ooo-er," she wailed.
"I don't like this!"
She stretched out
a paw and . . .

89

WHOOPS!

knocked some honeycomb to the ground.

A bee stung her
angrily on the nose.

"Ouch!"

Then Figgy found she was stuck.
"Help!" she cried. "I'm stuck!"

But nobody heard.

Jefferson Bear was going home that night when he heard someone whimpering.

"Help! Help! Help! Help!"

"Is that you, Figgy?" he called.

"Please help me down, JB," said Figgy.

As soon as she reached the ground, she took some honeycomb and ran off to find Buncle. "Wait there, JB!" she called.

Figgy Twosocks ran back, carrying the tickling stick.

"You've found it!" exclaimed Jefferson Bear.

Figgy's nose began to twitch.

"Figgy," said JB, "your nose is going all twitchy again. Is there something you want to tell me?"

Figgy Twosocks told JB everything.

"I was too scared to tell you before," she whispered.

"Too scared to tell your friend, but not too scared to climb a tree," said Jefferson Bear.

"I'm sorry, JB," said Figgy. "Will you forgive me?"

"I forgive you," said Jefferson Bear.
"Now, let's have that midnight feast."